The Very Little
Princess
Rose's Story

The Very Little
Princess
Rose's Story

by Marion Dane Bauer

illustrated by Elizabeth Sayles

Random House 🏠 New York

For my dear Katy
—M.D.B.

For Jessica
—E.S.

Text copyright © 2011 by Marion Dane Bauer
Jacket art and interior illustrations copyright © 2011 by Elizabeth Sayles

Visit us on the Web!
SteppingStonesBooks.com
www.randomhouse.com/kids

Educators and librarians, for a variety of teaching tools, visit us at
www.randomhouse.com/teachers

Library of Congress Cataloging-in-Publication Data
Bauer, Marion Dane.
The very little princess : Rose's story / by Marion Dane Bauer ; illustrated by Elizabeth Sayles. — 1st ed.
p.   cm. — (A Stepping Stone book)
Summary: After discovering a tiny, delicate china doll in an old trunk, Rose is amazed when the doll comes to life, claiming to be a princess, and starts ordering Rose about.
ISBN 978-0-375-85692-1 (trade) — ISBN 978-0-375-95692-8 (lib. bdg.) — ISBN 978-0-375-85694-5 (pbk.) — ISBN 978-0-375-89822-8 (ebook)
[1. Dolls—Fiction.]   I. Sayles, Elizabeth, ill. II. Title.
PZ7.B3262Ver 2011   [Fic]—dc22   2010030127

Printed in the United States of America
10 9 8 7 6 5 4 3 2 1

Contents

Chapter 1

"I'll Take Care of Her!"

Once upon a time . . .

That's the way stories begin, isn't it? *Once upon a time.* At least that's the way *this* story begins.

Once upon a time, there was a girl and a doll.

Actually, there was one doll and several different girls, because dolls always stay the same, while girls have a way of growing up and not being girls any longer.

This story is, however, about one moment in time and one particular girl. Her name was Rose.

Rose found the doll in the attic. She had gone there looking for dress-up clothes, something fit for the princess she was pretending to be. What she found, tucked away in a dark corner at the very bottom of a trunk, was the doll.

The doll was tiny. (Rose measured her later with the ruler she kept in her desk at school. She was exactly three and one-quarter inches tall.)

She was made of fine china. Her face was very white and very smooth. Her cheeks were touched with pink.

She wore a flouncy pink gown and lacy pantaloons, and she had a teeny pink bow in her hair. Her eyes were blue. Her hair was spun gold. Rose had never seen spun gold. But if anybody had managed to spin gold, she was sure the doll's hair was exactly the color it would be.

In other words, the doll was perfect.

The truth is that before that moment, Rose hadn't liked dolls all that much. They have a way of sitting around staring at you that she had never cared for. But *this* doll seemed different.

It was her eyes, for one thing. They looked down and away, as if she might be hiding something. Rose wanted to know, instantly, what a doll could have to hide.

Then there was her expression. It wasn't the usual "aren't I cute?" doll look. Instead, it seemed to say, "Who do you think you are, putting your hands all over me?"

Some girls might find such a look off-putting, especially on a very small doll. But

Rose felt a pang of sympathy. That was the way *she* felt sometimes, too. A snuggle in her dad's strong arms or her mom's pillowy ones felt as right as rain. But once when that old lady at church had spat on a tissue and wiped something off Rose's cheek, Rose had spat back.

Her parents had scolded her all the way home over that one.

But back to the doll.

She was perfect and . . . well, let's admit it, easy to tuck away into a pocket. So Rose did. She thrust the tiny doll into her pocket and climbed back down the attic steps.

Now, Rose wasn't hiding the doll, exactly. At least, she had no plans for keeping it secret. But she wasn't thinking about showing her mother what she had found, either.

After all, why had the doll been tucked away in the bottom of a trunk? Did Hazel, Rose's mother, sneak up to the attic to play with her after everyone else had gone to bed? Was the tiny thing a surprise being kept for Sam, Rose's big brother?

Rose smiled at the thought. (Sam was the star player on the high school football team. He would never play with dolls!)

So when Hazel appeared on the second-floor landing carrying a laundry basket at the same moment Rose stepped down into the hallway, Rose didn't think of herself as caught. She hadn't, after all, been doing anything wrong. But she couldn't help laying her hand over the small bulge in her pocket.

Hazel's face was flushed from climbing the stairs. Her blue eyes searched Rose's face, then her hand. "What do you have there?" she asked.

"Nothing," Rose replied, too brightly, perhaps, to be believed.

"Nothing?" Her mother's eyebrows rose.

"Nothing," Rose repeated. As if to prove her point, she let her hand fall away from the pocket.

"What's that, then?" Hazel asked. She set the basket down and nodded toward the place where Rose's hand had been.

Rose looked down. The doll was so small, she barely made a bump. What showed was

the flouncy pink gown. A bit of it poked out at the top of her pocket.

"Oh, that," Rose said. And instantly, her imagination took flight. Rose's imagination was good at flying.

"It's a handkerchief I found," she said. "A pretty one. But it's full of snot now. My nose has been awfully snotty lately. Has your nose been snotty, too?"

Before Hazel could answer, Rose tumbled on. "I've got some other stuff in there." She tugged at the top of her pocket and peered in. "There's broccoli. Kind of squished. You gave me too much broccoli last night at dinner. And . . . and, oh . . ." She patted her pocket. "There's a dog turd, too. I found it in Mrs. Ratchet's yard, and I thought she'd be happy if I picked it up. It's only a small one, of course, because Mrs. Ratchet's dog is kind of—"

"Rose!" Hazel interrupted. And she held out a hand for whatever might be in that pocket. Considering the list she'd just been given, it was a brave thing to do.

Rose hesitated. She wasn't a girl who gave in easily. Still, with her mother's hand waiting like that, there wasn't much else she could do. She reached into her pocket and pulled out the tiny doll. She didn't give it over, though. She just held it flat on her palm for her mother to see.

"Oh!" Hazel's hands flew to her round cheeks. "Oh!" she said again. Then she added, with what seemed great certainty, "You don't want *that*!"

"I do," Rose answered. Her certainty was every bit as great.

"But you don't *like* dolls," Hazel argued. She couldn't seem, herself, to take her eyes off this one.

"I like *this* doll," Rose told her, still holding it out. "I like it a lot."

Apparently Hazel didn't know what to say to that. She just stood staring at the tiny pink and white doll in Rose's hand.

"Where did it come from?" Rose asked. And then she asked the even larger question that had been burning in the exact center of her chest since she had plucked the china figure from the trunk. "Why was it hidden away?"

Hazel lifted her gaze to Rose's face. "I put her away to keep her safe," she said finally.

"Safe?" Rose asked. "Who were you keeping her safe from?" But she knew. Of course she knew.

"I didn't want her to get broken," Hazel said.

"You were afraid *I* would break her?" Rose spoke softly.

For a long moment, Hazel closed her eyes. When she opened them again, she said, "Yes.

I was afraid you would break her." Her tone was honest, resigned, a bit weary.

In that wait for an answer, as much as from the answer itself, Rose understood what she hadn't before. This doll was important. Too important for her.

Rose was a thousand things I've not yet had a chance to tell you. She was intelligent and imaginative and loads of fun. She was reckless and irrepressible and could swing from high joy to fury in an instant . . . before dropping into silent despair.

And she might have been one of the most careless girls who ever walked the earth.

She knew that about herself. Dishes seemed to leap from her hands to break. Pencils snapped. Homework was completed and then left on the school playground to blow in the wind.

She'd lost her brother's goldfish down the

toilet once. She never could explain quite how that had happened.

All of which meant that she knew a tiny doll made out of china could never be safe in her hands. She knew that to be true, but she didn't want it to be true. Which was, of course, precisely why she had to have the doll.

So instead of giving her up as Hazel's steady gaze demanded, Rose curled her fingers around the tiny thing. Or she started to.

Even as Rose's hand began to close, Hazel reached for the doll.

What followed wasn't Rose's fault. Not really. Their hands just bumped. Right there at the top of the stairs, her mother's hand and hers knocked into one another.

The doll flipped out of Rose's palm. She turned a somersault in the air. She flew over the banister.

Then she dropped like a pebble to the floor
below.

There! Rose said to herself. *Now Mom doesn't have to be afraid anymore. It's done. I've broken it.*

Still . . . she dashed down the stairs to see what had happened.

When Rose reached the floor below, where the doll had landed, she knelt on the rug. How lucky that there was a rug! She picked up the tiny doll. She smoothed the gauzy pink gown and the golden hair.

She ran her fingers along the doll's arms and legs. She touched the delicate china face.

Incredibly, nothing was broken. Not yet, anyway.

Rose looked up at Hazel, leaning over the banister. Her mother's face was stricken. Rose held the doll up to show that it was whole.

But then Rose cupped the doll in her hands and folded it tightly against her chest. "She's mine," she said. "All mine. I'll take care of her!"

Chapter 2

Show-and-Tell

Rose and her mother didn't speak of the doll for the rest of the day. Sometimes they had days like that, when silence filled all the space between them. Other days they chattered back and forth about everything from the silken weight of the spring air to whether to have chicken or spaghetti for dinner.

This time it was impossible to tell if the silence began with Hazel or with Rose. Perhaps it grew from both sides at once.

Rose, for her part, was full of questions she

didn't dare ask. *Where did the doll come from? Had it once belonged to Hazel? Had it ever had a name? Was it valuable? Would her mother have blamed her if the doll had broken?*

So with all those questions bumbling around inside her head unspoken, Rose didn't ask if she could take the doll to school the next day.

Why ask? If she had waited for her mother to tell her anything, she wouldn't have known that the doll existed. And then she never could have had her tucked inside her desk at school on show-and-tell day.

Drag-and-brag was what her teacher, Mr. Simmons, called it. Rose had never taken part in show-and-tell before. She didn't like standing in front of the class and being stared at. But this doll was different from anything else Rose had ever owned. She wanted everyone to know she had something so fine.

Not only was the doll special, but having the doll made her special, too. Surely the other kids would see that!

When the time came for show-and-tell, Mr. Simmons called on Jacob Flesner first. He'd brought the Purple Heart his grandfather had been awarded as a soldier in Vietnam. Everybody was impressed . . . with the medal on its purple ribbon, with Jacob for having such a brave grandfather.

The kids passed the medal around solemnly. Jacob looked solemn, too. Even the medal looked solemn.

Stephanie Crane brought a photo of the Corn Palace in Mitchell, South Dakota. Her family had visited the Corn Palace—and the Badlands and the Black Hills, too—during spring break.

Mr. Simmons asked Stephanie if she'd

enjoyed the trip. She said her butt was still sore from riding in the car for so long.

Everybody laughed when she said *butt*, and Stephanie blushed. She wasn't the kind of girl who said *butt* . . . not in front of the teacher.

Then it was Rose's turn.

Jacob's grandfather's Purple Heart and Stephanie's photo of the Corn Palace were still passing from desk to desk when Rose walked to the front of the room. She held the tiny doll close against her stomach. She turned to face the class.

They gazed back at her, all of them waiting.

And that was when one of the boys dropped Jacob's granddad's Purple Heart on the floor. It clanked loudly.

"Be careful!" Jacob cried.

In another part of the room someone grabbed Stephanie's photo from someone else.

The photo didn't tear, but Rose saw it bend.

Photos could be replaced. At least new photos could. And Stephanie's family probably had lots of pictures of the Corn Palace anyway. Maybe Purple Hearts could be replaced, too. Rose wasn't sure about that. But this one didn't seem to be breakable.

Suddenly Rose didn't want anyone to touch her doll.

She wasn't even sure she wanted anyone to see it!

So she turned abruptly and headed back to her desk.

"Rose?" Mr. Simmons asked. "Where are you going?"

"I changed my mind," she said. "I don't want to do show-and-tell." And she sat down.

A boy in the back of the room laughed . . . loudly. Two girls, right in front of her, rolled

their eyes at one another. (Their names were
Dawn and Melanie, but Rose liked to think of
them as Dumb and Meanie.) They did that a
lot . . . acted as if she weren't there, as if she
couldn't see them roll their eyes.

Rose knew what it all meant. She was being funny again. Not funny "ha-ha." Funny odd. The kind of funny that made girls whisper and giggle behind their hands. The kind that made boys dance on the playground and spin their index fingers at their temples and call out names . . . *nutcase* . . . *weirdo*.

Rose had never understood what she did to earn the whispers, the giggles, the names. She knew she couldn't talk in the same easy way other kids did. Her words either came out in a tumble, too many at once, or they didn't come out at all. And when it was time for gym class, she was all elbows and knees. She certainly couldn't hit a home run for her team or impress anyone by doing the most jumping jacks.

She was smart enough. She knew that. Sam had taught her to read before she'd even started school, and she could do math as well as anybody. She could make up stories that even the kids who teased her liked to hear.

But she didn't care how odd they thought she was to change her mind. She wasn't going to turn her doll over to their dirty, careless hands!

"Rose!" Mr. Simmons said again.

He seemed to think that, like a dog, when she heard her name spoken very sharply she would obey.

She didn't answer, and a nervous titter ran through the class. The boy in the back of the room laughed loudly again.

"I think you should come up here," Mr. Simmons said. "We want to see what's in your hand."

By this time, Rose had slipped the doll inside her desk. She laid it down gently on top of her math book.

"I haven't got anything in my hand, Mr. Simmons." She held both hands up, splayed and empty.

Mr. Simmons had been sitting behind his desk, and now he stood. He was tall and thin and angular, rather like Ichabod Crane. Ichabod Crane was a character in a story Rose had read. She liked the story better than she liked Mr. Simmons.

"Then you should come up here," he said, "and tell us about what you just put inside your desk." He took a step toward Rose.

Perhaps it's worth noting that all the bullies in school aren't on the playground . . . or sitting in the students' desks. But you, no doubt, already know this.

Rose, however, wasn't going to be bullied. She had never been much for letting people tell her what to do. "I changed my mind," she said again.

"Then change it back," Mr. Simmons snapped. He had come to stand beside Rose's desk. "You don't participate enough in class."

Why it mattered so much to him, I don't know. Maybe because Rose, sitting there silently day after day, made him feel like a failure. It's never good to make a teacher feel like a failure.

It was, in any case, the kind of situation adults sometimes get caught in. Once he'd started, Mr. Simmons couldn't back down. If he did, the whole class might quit listening to him.

And we all know what a wretched thing school would be if no one listened to the teacher. More boring even than the most boring work sheet.

Mr. Simmons laid a hand on Rose's shoulder. He pressed down just a bit too hard.

"Leave me alone!" Rose cried. She stood up so suddenly that Mr. Simmons's hand fell away.

And to her own dismay, tears sprang to her eyes. It was as if a faucet she wasn't in charge of had been turned on.

No one was more amazed at the tears than Rose. She rarely cried. Not in front of teachers. Not in front of other kids, either.

She slapped at the annoying drops pouring down her face. Ignoring the look on Mr. Simmons's face, she reached into her desk, grabbed the doll in her damp hand, and headed for the door.

As she moved up the aisle, though, something strange happened.

The doll moved in her hand.

Now, Rose knew better, of course. Dolls don't move . . . unless they come with a battery or a windup key. And this one had neither. But it didn't matter what Rose knew. The doll moved anyway.

It was a wriggle. Or maybe it was a series of small jerks. Certainly it wasn't anything you would expect from a china doll.

If a doll suddenly moved in my hand, I'd probably drop it in surprise. I'll bet you would, too.

But Rose didn't flinch. She simply tightened her hand over the wriggle.

And then, just as she pushed through the door to the hall, a voice rang out from the hollow of her hand. "What do you think you're doing?" the voice said. "Put me down this instant!"

Chapter 3

"Your Royal Highness"

When Rose reached the sidewalk in front of the school, she didn't stop to examine the doll. She just ran, her fingers wrapped tightly around the squirming, shouting little thing.

She kept running until she had a stitch in her side. Even then she didn't slow down much. She just pressed her free hand into the pain and kept going.

"What do you think you're doing?" the tiny doll said again. And she added, "You big . . ."

That was followed by a string of what were obviously meant to be swear words. They seemed to be the tiny doll's own invention . . . or else they were in another language. Either way, Rose had never heard any of the words before.

Rose ran until she reached her own house, a tall yellow one set well back from a gravel road. When she got there, she didn't go to the door, though.

She didn't want her mother to see her. Hazel was understanding about many things. She understood that sitting still in school wasn't easy for a girl like Rose. She even understood that Mr. Simmons could be annoying. But running out of school in the middle of the day with her teacher bellowing behind her . . . Hazel wouldn't understand that. In fact, she would be very upset.

And Rose didn't think there was a grown-up

in the world who would understand a three-and-a-quarter-inch doll that wriggled and swore!

So she scurried along the side of the house toward the best hiding spot she knew. It was the weeping willow tree at the very back of the yard. Even though it was early spring, the willow had already put on its dressing of slender leaves. The pale branches trailed on the ground on every side, making the tree a perfect hiding spot.

Rose ducked beneath the tree and threw herself down on the mossy ground, her heart pounding. She opened her hand slowly.

The china doll lying in her palm was very damp, very rumpled, and very, very angry. She sat up and went right on yelling, if the small, shrill voice coming from such a tiny throat could be called yelling.

"What do you think you're doing?" she

asked for the third time, and she kicked her heels against Rose's palm.

"I'm keeping you safe!" Rose snapped.

"Safe from what?" the doll said. "Big, clumsy oafs who block out the sun?"

Rose opened her mouth. As you've probably noticed, she was usually quick with answers. But her mouth closed again before anything came out. She did feel like a big, clumsy oaf next to this tiny thing. Who wouldn't?

And besides, a million questions swirled in her brain.

The most important one was . . . how had this happened? When Rose had tucked her find into her pocket in the attic, the doll had been a doll. When she had watched it drop over the banister, it was just a doll. When she had brought it to school that morning and placed it in her desk on her math book, the doll had been a doll. Nothing more.

But now the china doll moved her arms and legs and turned her head. She stood in Rose's hand and plopped back down again.

Even her face changed. Her eyes widened. Her mouth opened and closed . . . and pouted. And, of course, she talked. Her shrill voice practically cleaned the wax out of Rose's ears.

She wasn't exactly *alive*, if being alive means being flesh and blood. She was still made of china. But she was certainly *awake*.

Rose picked the doll up between her thumb and forefinger. She set her down on a mossy rock at the base of the willow tree and stared at her.

A three-and-one-quarter-inch doll that walked and talked! Nothing so wonderful had ever happened to Rose in her entire life!

So instead of wading into an argument,

which would have been easy to do, she bowed
deeply. "Your Royal Highness," she said, "I am
your humble servant."

Rose didn't really mean it, you understand.
Or rather she only half meant it. Mostly she
was repeating something Sam sometimes said
to her. Usually it was when he'd decided she'd
gotten "the big head."

But apparently the doll didn't know that. She crossed her tiny arms over her tiny chest and looked Rose in the eye. "Well," she said, "it's about time somebody realized who I am!"

Have you ever gazed up at the underside of a weeping willow tree from the point of view of a three-and-one-quarter-inch doll?

Of course you haven't. But imagine it. The leaves tremble in the breeze, forming a wall of shimmering green. The branches curving above you are the ceiling of a palace.

You sink deep into a cushion of velvet moss. The rock you're sitting on becomes a throne.

And this girl, this enormous girl with a great snarl of dark curls, has just bowed to you. She has said the words that you have always known were yours to hear, "Your Royal Highness" and "I am your humble servant."

What would you say? What would you do?

Chances are pretty good that you would be more humble than this tiny doll. Most of us would be. But still, you might be tempted to take advantage of the moment . . . just a bit. And the doll was more than tempted.

"Every princess," she said in her most haughty voice, "should have flowers in her throne room. Why are there no flowers?"

Now, there are several very good reasons there were no flowers.

First, Rose hadn't known she would be entertaining a princess.

Second, few flowers can grow in the shade under a weeping willow tree.

And third, this was early spring in northern Minnesota. Flowers weren't growing much of anywhere yet.

The princess waited, but the giant girl who

had identified herself as a servant didn't apologize. She didn't run out to search for flowers, either, which is what any proper servant would have done. She simply sat and stared. Then she clapped her hands. And then she began to laugh, a great, rolling belly laugh. She obviously thought something was terribly funny.

"Throne room?" she cried. "Princess?" she howled. "You!"

The doll was speechless. Could this lug of a girl be making fun of her?

Impossible!

She was, as you have probably noticed, a very self-confident doll. But still, the laughter and the questions shocked her. If she wasn't a princess, who was she?

"Of course I'm a princess," the doll said. Doubting her own words made her speak even more emphatically. "I'm Princess . . ."

But she got no further. What was her name? Surely she had a name. Every princess did. She must have forgotten it while she slept.

The girl came to the princess's rescue . . . as a good servant should. "Princess Regina," Rose said, "how nice of you to come visit."

Now, just in case you don't know, *Regina* is a Latin word. It means *queen*. Being called Princess Regina is a bit like being called Princess Queen. Sam sometimes used the name to make fun of his over-the-top little sister. So now I know that and you know that. It just so happens that Rose knew it, too. But the doll didn't. In fact, she had no idea she was being teased. Princess Regina sounded quite fine to her. The instant she heard it, she was certain it had always been hers.

She tried the name on her tongue, softly. "Princess Regina," she said.

Then she looked up at the girl towering over her and frowned. She hardly seemed like a proper servant for a princess. Her dark too-curly hair poked in every direction at once.

And she had a smudge from a red marker on her cheek that she must have gotten at school. Even her shirt was buttoned wrong. She might have dressed with her eyes half closed.

Still, the princess made a decision. She couldn't remember where she had been before she woke in this girl's wet hand. But wherever it was, she didn't want to go back there. So she'd make the best of what she had at the moment. It was, I'm sure you'll agree, a wise choice.

She straightened her back and lifted her tiny chin. "It's not a visit," she said to the great moon face hovering above her. "You are much more fortunate than that. Princess Regina is here to stay!"

Chapter 4

Staying

And stay she did.

She stayed while Rose gathered pinecones and pebbles to decorate the throne room.

She stayed through the scolding. It seemed Rose's teacher had called. Regina wasn't much interested in what he'd had to say, since it had nothing to do with her. Rose's parents were certainly upset, though.

She stayed through dinner, perched on the edge of Rose's plate, pretending not to see or hear. She pretended, in fact, to be the lifeless china doll the grown-ups expected. She couldn't remember much from before she'd awakened in this enormous girl's hand. Still, she was pretty sure most adults got upset when they found out a doll could walk and talk.

And Princess Regina certainly stayed after Rose carried her upstairs to her room.

As soon as Rose closed the door, the princess began talking again.

She talked. And she talked. And she talked.

Rose listened.

After a while—it was a long time, really, but since Regina was doing most of the talking it didn't seem so long to her—Rose put on her pajamas and climbed into bed. She lifted Regina to the pillow and lay down next to her.

Princess Regina went on talking. Rose went on listening.

She talked about what it was like to be a

princess. It's a great responsibility, don't you know, to be in charge of such a huge world.

She talked about how difficult it was being small. ("I see the undersides of everything," she told Rose. "Including your nose. Ugh!")

She talked about what she wanted to do the next day. She wanted to go back to her throne room. She wanted Rose to find flowers, not just pebbles and pinecones. Surely there were flowers somewhere. She wanted Rose, her humble servant, to wait on her.

Rose talked a bit, too, mostly about Regina, which suited the little doll just fine. She admired Regina's pink and white cheeks, her golden hair, her sapphire eyes.

(*Sapphire* and *golden* and *pink* and *white* were instantly Regina's favorite colors.)

Rose's mother looked in a couple of times. Her father did, too. Regina went quiet when they appeared. When they were gone, she went back to talking.

But at the point that Regina began trying to remember former servants, all clumsy and oversized, too, Rose quit answering. Her eyes drifted closed.

How rude! Regina thought.

Rose began to breathe deeply.

"Wake up!" the princess ordered. She tugged on one of Rose's eyelashes. "I didn't say you could leave me!"

Rose's eyes popped open. Then they narrowed dangerously. "Don't you ever sleep?" she asked.

"Of course not!" Regina replied. "Why should I sleep?" She shuddered. She could think of few things she wanted less. That was where she had just come from, wasn't it? Sleep . . . or someplace very like it.

"Well," Rose said, "*I* do. Sleep, I mean. And if I'm not allowed to do it, I get to feeling real mean."

"So?" Regina said with a shrug of her tiny shoulders. Why should she care about how her servant *felt*?

But Rose wasn't through. "When I get to feeling mean"—she bared her teeth—"I eat little dolls!"

Eat! Little dolls! Princess Regina had never heard anything more silly . . . or more terrifying.

Still, she poked her chin out. "You can't eat me," she said. "I'm made of fine china. Nobody eats china."

She said this as though she were certain. But she wasn't entirely. Since she herself didn't eat, eating was something she didn't understand very well.

"Just try me!" Rose said. And she turned over, away from the tiny doll sitting on her pillow.

Regina decided not to.

She lay back on the pillow and let her humble servant drift off to sleep.

But while Rose slept, Regina sulked. She didn't like being alone. The girl had no right to leave her alone. No right at all.

She remembered the threat, though, about being eaten. So she waited, silent and still.

A smothering dark filled the room. It pressed in from every side.

The floor creaked. Had someone come in? Someone else who ate china dolls?

Moonlight stalked the floor. Every shape it found turned into a monster. Every monster was bigger than a thousand princess dolls. They were bigger than a hundred thousand dolls.

Regina closed her eyes to shut out the monsters. She could hear Rose breathing. She didn't know why humans had to breathe. It was an ugly sound.

She opened her eyes again.

More darkness.

After a long, long time the moonlight snuck away. The sky faded from black to navy blue. It went from navy blue to silver. Then it turned the palest pink possible.

Sunlight peeked in the bedroom window. Even when it lay across Rose's face, it didn't wake her. And Regina still didn't dare to.

The house came slowly to life with thumps and bumps.

Rose slept on.

At last Hazel's voice drifted up the stairs, riding on the smell of coffee and toast. "Rose," she called. "It's time to get up. Rose!"

The instant Rose's eyes opened, the little doll started talking again. Actually, she began complaining . . . loudly. "I don't know why you humans have to sleep so long," she said. "I don't understand why you have to sleep at all. A princess should never be left alone in the dark like that. It's creepy. And listening to you breathe . . . Ugh!"

Rose sat up and rubbed her eyes. She stared at Regina as though she'd forgotten she was there. "Don't you breathe?" she asked finally.

"No!" Regina said. "I don't breathe. And I don't eat. And I don't . . . well, I don't do that other thing you humans do. From the other end, you know?"

To Regina's surprise, Rose laughed. "La-di-da," she said. "Aren't you something?"

But before Regina could respond to that, Hazel called again. "Rose, dear! It's time to get up. School."

Rose's face went pale at the word *school*. Still, she called back, "I'm up." And she swung her feet out of the bed.

"I have to get ready," she told Regina. "And I can't take you with me this time. Something bad will happen if I do. Something bad nearly happened yesterday."

The only reason Princess Regina didn't go pale, too, was because she was made of china.

If she'd been made of blood and bones the way you and I are, her cheeks would certainly have lost their cheerful pink.

"You're going to go off and leave me!" she cried. "You're going to leave me alone after that horrible night?"

Rose shrugged. "I *have* to go to school. All kids do. It's a law . . . or something like that."

Princess Regina stood up in the middle of the pillow. She clenched her fists. She screwed her face into a ferocious frown. "You . . . will . . . not . . . leave . . . me!" she shouted. "And that's a command! If you're going to school, I will go to school, too. If you go out to play, I will play. If you eat, I will . . ." Here she hesitated. Then she started again. "I will watch you eat," she said. "But you won't leave me. Ever!"

Rose had been reaching for her clothes. She

stopped and turned back, her mouth fallen
open into an O.

Princess Regina waited. She would have
held her breath if she'd had breath to hold.
What would the girl do?

Regina was a princess. She knew she was a princess. Rose was her servant. That was certain. Servants followed orders. That was the way the world was made.

But even at her most royal, Regina could never quite forget that she was a very small princess. And this servant of hers was a very large girl.

Regina needn't have worried, though. Not right now, anyway.

Rose's mouth closed. It curled into a smile. It stretched into a grin. A laugh came tumbling out. "Well, then," she said, "if that's the way things are, I guess I'd better figure out how to hide you away!"

Relieved, Regina plopped down on the pillow. Everything would be all right! Rose was going to obey her.

Chapter 5

A World Shared

And she did. Rose tucked Regina safely into her pocket and kept her with her all day long.

The first thing she had to do when she got back to school was explain to Mr. Simmons why she had left so abruptly the day before.

And since she couldn't tell him that she couldn't stand his bullying, she had to make up a story. Luckily, Rose was good at stories.

"I got this terrible bellyache," she said. "It came on real fast. I didn't want to throw up on the clean school floor. So I decided I'd better get home right away."

When Mr. Simmons pointed out that he had called her mother and she hadn't known where Rose was, she added, "That's because I went around behind the house. I don't like to throw up in front of anybody, you see? It's the retching. The sound of it. It's so awful to listen to anybody retching. Don't you think? Whenever I hear that sound, it makes me want to—"

Mr. Simmons sent her to the principal, Ms. Whittenbottom. And at the exact same point in Rose's story, Ms. Whittenbottom sent her back to her classroom. Which was, of course, the next best thing to being sent home.

Dawn and Melanie, the girls who sat in front of Rose, had lots of practice rolling their eyes that day. They did it when Rose first came into the classroom. They did it when she was

52

explaining herself to Mr. Simmons. They did it when she was sent to the principal and when she came back.

They looked at one another across the desks each time and lifted their gaze to the ceiling. It was as if something odd about Rose were written there. Then they looked back at one another in that *meaningful* way again.

Their look said . . . well, you know exactly what it said. I don't need to explain.

Rose told herself she didn't care. She just set about creating a second throne room for the princess. Inside her desk she set her math and spelling books on one side. She stacked social studies and language arts on the other. She threw out all the old papers that filled the space between them and blew the crumbs off a fat pink eraser. It made a fine throne.

She even found a small notebook with some

blank pages and several broken crayons. (Most of Rose's crayons were broken.) Then she slipped Regina from her pocket, holding a finger to her lips to warn her to be still, and put her on the throne. She propped the desktop open a bit with another eraser to let in some light so the princess could draw.

With all that finished, Rose turned her attention to Mr. Simmons. He was at the chalkboard talking about adjectives. Rose pretended to be extremely interested in adjectives.

Strangely, the day whizzed by. Having a tiny princess in her desk made every moment more interesting. Or if lessons about adjectives weren't exactly interesting, they passed more quickly than usual.

Rose kept slipping her hand into her desk to make sure Regina was really there. Had she dreamed her? No! There she was!

This was what she had needed all her life, a tiny, walking, talking doll made out of china. She just hadn't known it before now.

Each time Rose reached for Regina, the doll touched her. She tapped a fingernail or ran a china finger across Rose's wrist. The touch was hard—hard as china—and cold—cold as china, too—but every single time it made Rose glow.

When the school bell rang, Rose tucked Regina into her pocket again and hurried home. When she got there, though, she didn't go in. She waved to her mother, who was watering her plants at the living room window, and headed for the woods behind the house.

There they walked and talked. At least Rose walked. The princess rode and gave directions.

"Let's climb that tree." (One bottom limb

of an old oak tree dipped almost to the ground, so Rose simply walked up it. If the princess was impressed, she didn't say so.)

"Are you brave enough to cross that fierce river?" (It was a bubbling creek, and Rose was.)

"Look! Flowers! I told you I needed flowers." (Shy snowdrops, but they wilted almost as soon as Rose picked them.)

Rose made it back to the house just barely in time for dinner. What a day it had been! Wasn't it amazing how fine the world could be when it was shared?

"Did something good happen today?" her dad asked, studying her beaming face.

Rose smiled and nodded, but she didn't try to explain. What could she say? Regina sat on the edge of her plate and was silent, too.

When Rose went upstairs to her room and shut the door, however, the argument began.

"You aren't going to sleep again tonight, are you?" Regina asked.

Something about the question made Rose cross. "Of course I'm going to sleep," she said. "I sleep every night. Just like I eat every day. And I breathe, too. And I'm going to go on breathing. Every single minute." She plopped the princess down on her bed, a little harder than she needed to.

"What's wrong with you humans?" Regina shouted in her shrill voice. "Don't you know better than—"

Rose looked up to see Sam standing in her doorway. He'd been late for dinner and held a plate in one hand, heaped with mashed potatoes and chicken and peas. "What's going on, pip-squeak?" he asked.

"Nothing," Rose replied. She snatched Regina up and whipped her behind her back.

"It sounds like a regular ruckus." Sam licked mashed potatoes off a chicken leg and took a big bite. His gaze traveled the room.

He'd missed dinner the last couple of nights because of baseball practice, so Rose hadn't yet had a chance to show him the doll. This hardly seemed the time for introductions, though.

Sam leaned against the doorjamb, filling the doorway. He was tall and big-shouldered and . . . Well, everything about him was the giant economy size. He had a bush of tangled curls, very much like Rose's.

His dark eyes searched her face. Clearly he was waiting for a better answer than "nothing."

Rose tried again. "I was just . . . ah . . . I was practicing for the school play. I'm going to be a mouse, you know. One that gets its tail caught in a trap?" And she made her voice high and thin. "What's wrong with you humans?"

she squeaked. "Don't you know better—"

Sam laughed. Rose liked to make her brother laugh. His laugh was deep and as generously sized as he was.

He took another bite of the chicken but didn't take his eyes off her face. "What's that behind your back?" he asked.

"Behind my back?" Rose repeated. Even she could hear how guilty she sounded. Her voice squeaked again on the word *back*.

Sam said nothing. He just put the chicken leg down, wiped his fingers on his pants, and held out his hand. Rose barely hesitated before she gave up. She could often fool her father, sometimes her mother, but never Sam.

"It's just this old doll," she said. She held Princess Regina out without letting go of her. She hoped the silly thing would stay quiet a bit longer. "I found her in the attic. And I was playing with her, talking for her, you know?

The way *little kids* do." She leaned heavily on *little kids* because she wanted Sam to see how unimportant it all was. Something for little kids, not for a big boy like him.

Princess Regina, for her part, seemed to have entered into the game. She lay rigidly in Rose's hand as if she'd gone to sleep again. Rose was pretty sure the doll was faking. At least she hoped she was.

But instead of glancing at her hand and then away again, Sam leaned close. His eyebrows rose until they practically vanished into his dark curls. "You've found Princess Regina!" he said.

Rose started to nod, but she stopped cold. *Princess Regina?* Sam had called the doll *Princess Regina!* She hadn't told him the doll's name. She hadn't told *anyone.*

"How do you know she's Princess Regina?" Rose demanded.

"The same way you know, I'm sure," he replied. "*She* told me."

Rose was going to set the record straight. The doll hadn't given herself the name. Rose had come up with it herself!

But before she could, the princess sat up in Rose's hand. She looked at Sam and cried, "Why, Sammy! Just look at you. You've gotten to be enormous!"

Chapter 6

"Prickly as a Porcupine"

The three of them sat together in the middle of the floor, talking. Rose told Sam everything while Princess Regina kept interrupting.

Rose told Sam how she'd found the doll in the bottom of the trunk.

Princess Regina said, "I don't know what took you so long. You humans are so slow. I must have been in that stuffy trunk forever."

Rose told about the way her mother's hand

and hers had knocked into one another, sending the doll over the banister.

Princess Regina cried, "You dropped me? You mean you actually dropped me? What a klutz! You're lucky I wasn't broken."

(Rose wondered why *she* was the lucky one. After all, it was *Regina* who didn't get broken.)

Rose told Sam about taking the doll to school for show-and-tell and about how she decided not to show her after all.

Princess Regina said, "What a shame. I'm sure the children would have been impressed."

Then Rose explained how Regina came alive in her hand as she ran out of the classroom.

Princess Regina added, "And she was crying. Would you believe it? I thought I was going to drown in her stupid tears."

Now Rose got to the part about naming the doll. While she was telling that, a thought struck her. "The name I gave her—Princess Regina—it came from you!"

"No." Sam grinned. "It came from *her*." He nodded toward the doll, who was perched on the toe of his sneaker. "She told me her name was Princess Regina a long time ago."

Rose shook her head, trying to clear the jumble of her thoughts. "But," she pointed out to Sam, "you used to call *me* that!"

Sam shrugged. "What can I say? I'm not good at making things up the way you are. I named you after the only other princess I knew."

"And then I gave the name back to her!" Rose said, amazed at the circle of events.

"I told you," Princess Regina said. "You didn't *give* me anything. Don't you think I know my own name?" And she went on like that.

(You and I know, of course, that when Regina first woke she had forgotten her name entirely. So Rose actually *did* give it to her, even if the name had belonged to her before. But you can bet the princess would never admit that.)

Rose shook her head and smiled at Sam over the fuming doll. He grinned back.

Rose loved her brother so much that sometimes just looking at him made her heart ache.

"How did you know about the doll?" she asked finally. "Did you find her in the attic, too?"

Sam touched Princess Regina's spun-gold hair. "Mom gave her to me," he said, "when I was a little kid. Younger than you. I'm sure she'd been hoping to have a daughter to give her to. But she'd been waiting a long time. I guess she decided I'd have to do."

Rose ducked her head. She loved thinking about her mother hoping for her, waiting for her. She wasn't sure she had lived up to all that waiting and hoping, though . . . or ever would.

Then she thought about the fact that Hazel had given Princess Regina to Sam when he was younger than she was now. And yet she had never brought the doll out for her. Even when Rose had found Regina in the attic, her mother had clearly not wanted her to have her.

Rose shook those thoughts away. To Sam she said, "So Princess Regina came awake for you, too?"

"No," he said. "Not at first. When Mom gave her to me, she was just a doll. And I wasn't much interested in dolls, you know?"

Rose grinned. The very thought of her big brother playing with a tiny china doll was funny.

"I played with her a little bit," he said. "I used to give her rides in my race cars when they were going very slowly . . . no crashes. Then I put her on a shelf in my room so nothing bad would happen to her. I knew she was important to Mom. I didn't pay much attention to her after that until . . ." But he didn't say until when.

Rose stared up into Sam's face. "What happened?" she asked.

Sam lifted his great shoulders and let them fall again. "I'm not sure. One afternoon I had a fight with my buddy Brian. A pretty bad one. Fists and a bloody nose. Brian's nose, not mine."

He stopped as if he wasn't going to say more, but when neither Rose nor Regina spoke, he started again. "I came home to hole up in my room, and I took the doll off the shelf. I don't know why, exactly. I was feeling awful, and I just needed something to mess with. I guess I was kind of blubbering. Then—I never knew what happened—there she was, talking to me, walking all over me, telling me what to do and how to do it. I was . . ."

He stopped, looked hard at Regina, and let out a low laugh. "*Surprised* isn't a big enough word for what I was. I never understood how it happened. All I knew was that I was there, alone in my room feeling pretty bad, and suddenly I had this big *secret*. The little doll Mom had trusted to me could move. She could talk, too! Yell, actually."

Rose could see the moment exactly. Hadn't it happened to her in almost the same way? She loved that! She and her big brother shared a secret, the best secret ever!

"I couldn't tell anybody," Sam said. "I sure couldn't go back to school and tell my buddies that I had a little dolly at home that walked and talked." He ran his fingers through his curls and shook his head. "I almost told Mom, but then . . . Well, what could I say? 'This little doll you gave me, she's a princess, you know' . . . ? I didn't think even Mom would . . ."

Again, he stopped.

A late-to-bed robin chirruped outside the window. The robin fell silent, too.

Rose nodded. It was so comforting to know that Sam had felt the same way.

"So," Sam continued, "the next day I made up with Brian. Then I invited him to come home with me after school. I wanted to let him see for himself."

"And did he see?" Rose asked.

Sam shook his head. "When we got back here . . . there she was. She was sitting on the bed where I'd left her. And she was . . . nothing. She was just a doll again. You know? It didn't matter how hard I shook her. Or what I said. She wouldn't say a word."

He grinned sheepishly. "Brian and I had another fight. He told me I was full of it, talking to a stupid doll. I punched him again."

Rose let out the breath she hadn't even known she'd been holding. "Was that the last time?" she asked. "Not you and Brian. Princess Regina. Did she ever . . . ?"

"Never," he said. "That was the last time. And after that . . . not long after that, I guess, I gave her back to Mom. I told her the doll was nice and all, but I didn't want her. Mom was kind of sad, I could tell, but she took her back. And I never saw her again."

"Until now," Rose said.

"Until now," he agreed. "I even got to thinking I'd dreamed the whole thing. It was so strange. And it lasted such a short time." He paused to study Regina, then turned his gaze to Rose. "It's really important that nobody knows about this. No other kids, no adults, either. Bad things will happen if people find out . . . bad things for *her*." He pointed to the tiny doll.

What kind of bad things? Rose wondered, but she knew. The world wasn't ready for china dolls that could walk and talk. Certainly the world wasn't ready for a three-and-one-quarter-inch princess!

"What do you think makes her go to sleep

again," Rose asked, "after she's been awake?"

"I think she likes messing with us," Sam answered without missing a beat. "I think she's prickly as a porcupine and likes messing with us."

Rose laughed. That perfectly described what she'd already seen of Regina.

Apparently Princess Regina wasn't equally pleased with the description, though. She pushed herself off the toe of Sam's sneaker and stomped her feet in the carpet. And then, probably because feet that are only a quarter of an inch long make no sound at all when stomped in carpet, she tipped her head back and howled, "I am not prickly!"

Though, of course, you and I know better.

Now, I've never been a three-and-one-quarter-inch doll myself, but I'd guess being prickly would be easy if you were that small.

Think about it. You would be so tiny that people could pick you up and put you down wherever they chose . . . *when*ever they chose, too.

Even worse, if they weren't paying close attention, they might not see you at all.

And perhaps that was why Regina needed to be prickly. Folks would be forced to pay attention.

So she stomped her foot in the soft carpet and howled, "I am not prickly!" And then she added, as though it explained everything—and perhaps it did—"I am a princess!"

Chapter 7

Into the Green and Blooming Summer

And a princess she remained. But being a princess didn't keep her from having a good time. In fact, Regina couldn't remember ever having as much fun as she had with her new servant, as oddly unreliable as Rose was.

Rose could come up with the most amazing adventures.

One night, as Regina lay on the pillow next to Rose, bored with this silly sleeping business, she was amazed to see the girl suddenly sit up. Rose studied the fat-faced moon peering through her window. Then she got out of bed, tucked Regina into the elastic of her pajamas, and crawled out her second-floor bedroom window.

Regina closed her eyes as Rose swung from the sill. "Remember," she cried, "I break!"

But Rose just caught hold of the trellis leaning against the wall and climbed down to the moon-washed grass. Once there, she held the princess high in the air and danced and danced.

When she tried to climb the trellis to go back to her room, though, it broke under her weight. She had to go around to the front porch and ring the bell to get back in.

Rose's dad came to the door looking bed-rumpled and bewildered and even a bit cross. (Her dad was rarely cross.) Still, Rose giggled, and Regina couldn't help but join in . . . very quietly.

Rose came up with adventures during the day, too. After school or on weekends, they explored the woods behind Rose's house again and again.

They climbed back into the attic to search for more treasure. (The closest they found to treasure was an old teddy bear, leaking sawdust. Regina was glad when Rose put him back into the trunk. He was awfully big. What if he decided to come awake . . . and bite?)

They checked out the town, too.

They stopped at the empty school playground. Rose would sit on a swing, wind it up, then let it spin until even Regina was dizzy.

They peered through the windows of the grocery store and the drugstore and Kathi's Kut and Kurl.

But better than anything else were their visits to the hardware store. It wasn't the bins of screws and the cans of paint that drew them. It wasn't even the balls and scooters and dolls that never woke. It was the dollhouse sitting all by itself on a shelf in the back of the store.

The instant she saw it, Regina fell in love.
How could she not? Everything about it was
sized for her!

Upstairs the house had a bedroom and a
bathroom, though, of course, Princess Regina
did *not* need a bathroom.

Downstairs held a living room and a kitchen. She didn't *need* a kitchen, either, but Regina rather liked this one anyway.

Rose wouldn't let Regina go inside, though, no matter how much she begged. "Someone might come back here and see you," she'd whisper. "And then there'd be trouble."

Regina knew Rose was right, but that didn't keep her from begging again the next time. She had never seen anything more wonderful than that little house, and by rights it should have been hers. She'd certainly not seen any human in town that it would fit. And what good would a little house be to any of those sleeping dolls that sat on the shelves nearby?

They talked about the dollhouse so much that even Sam went with them once to see it.

"If I had that house, I'd be happy forever," Regina said.

"Would you?" Sam asked, giving her a considering look. "Even if Rose wasn't right there every minute, paying attention?"

"Of course," the princess said. She tossed her golden hair. "Why would I need Rose if I had my own house?"

But that was the problem. Regina didn't have the little house, and she did need Rose. And while Rose was wondrously fun, she didn't always pay attention. In fact, sometimes she would set Regina down and forget her completely!

Sooner or later Rose always came back, but the princess found the wait annoying . . . even terrifying. "Someday," she warned Rose again and again, "you're going to come back and I'll be gone."

What she meant by *gone* she was never entirely sure. She knew only that what she said was true.

Then came an afternoon when they were sitting on the couch in the living room watching television. Regina didn't know why they were watching television. It was a beautiful blue day outside, and as far as she could tell, Rose wasn't paying any more attention to the TV than she was to her. She just kept flipping channels. She didn't even notice when Regina tumbled off her lap and dropped between the couch cushions.

"Get me out of here!" Regina cried. But

Rose didn't seem to hear her. Maybe Regina's voice was so squashed between the cushions that it couldn't escape.

Or maybe Rose was lost inside herself.

To make matters worse, Hazel called Rose to set the table for dinner. And off she went.

"My servant will come back for me," Regina promised herself. "She always does."

Regina was wrong, though. This time Rose didn't come back. Not even after supper.

The house grew heavy with silence. Princess Regina, in the cramped dark between the cushions, grew heavy, too. First her arms, then her legs seemed to fill with lead. If she'd been a breathing creature, she would have been struggling for air in the tight space. Fortunately, china dolls, even walking, talking ones, don't need air. But they need, as we all do, to be noticed.

The silence and dark pressed down on her

like a stone until she was herself a stone. She couldn't have moved or called out if Rose had suddenly plucked her from between the cushions into the bright air.

And that was when she fell into the empty place again.

Into dark silence.

Into nothingness.

Regina woke to find Rose crying all over her again.

"I'm sorry," Rose kept saying. "I'm really, really sorry. I thought I'd lost you forever. If Sam hadn't found you . . . I don't know what I would have done. And when he brought you back, you were gone. You were asleep. I was sure you were asleep!" And on and on.

Princess Regina wasn't just furious. She was disgusted. How could this girl be so careless, so thoughtless, so completely irresponsible?

"Why do I have to wake to such drama?" she asked. "Do you see me crying? And I'm the one who was wronged!"

(I must pause here. If you've read the first Very Little Princess book, you know more about this story than the story knows about itself. Which makes this moment rather awkward. I'll simply have to trust you to stay mum.)

For a while afterward, Rose kept Princess Regina close every moment. She was full of energy. She came up with new and wonderful games like dodge the raindrops. Regina loved that. Of course, she was better at it than Rose. But then, inevitably it seemed, the moment came when her servant forgot once more.

And then she forgot another time
and another
and another.

Sometimes Rose came back before the princess fell into sleep again, sometimes she didn't. Sometimes, if Regina had fallen asleep, she woke up the moment Rose found her, sometimes she didn't. The princess never did understand what this sleeping and waking business was about.

What she did understand was that this great girl was exceedingly careless.

Once Rose dropped Princess Regina in the cookie jar among the oatmeal raisin cookies. She left her on a dusty shelf in the basement. She even went off, forgetting Regina in the throne room. The princess had to sit watching the dark creep between the whispering leaves of the willow tree.

The worst, though, was when Rose left her in her desk at school over an entire weekend. The princess couldn't believe anyone could do such a thing. First the sharp sound of the bell, desks slamming, feet smacking the floor. But no hand reaching in to carry her home.

Then quiet, the slow slap of Mr. Simmons's long, narrow feet moving around the room, the door closing, the door locking.

When Regina heard it open again, she was elated. Rose had remembered! She'd come back before it was too late! The princess already had a good, stern lecture composed in her mind.

But it was only the janitor, sweeping the floor. And then the silence . . . the terrible silence.

The deep sleep came very soon after.

Rose went off and left Princess Regina so many times and in so many places that the doll couldn't keep track of them all, even when she tried to call up a list of Rose's offenses to shout at her.

She only knew that she woke, every time,

to the mess of Rose's tears. And every time she was furious.

Rose always said she was sorry. She seemed to mean it, too. She promised that she would never leave her tiny charge again, not even for an instant. But Rose was Rose, and promises had a way of not holding.

So the girl and the doll bumped through to the end of the school year, sometimes remembering, sometimes forgetting, sometimes awake, sometimes asleep. Sometimes they could barely stand one another. Sometimes they were the best of friends. And that was the way they emerged into the green and blooming summer.

Chapter 8

"Ding-Dong Drat It!"

It was a fine June morning. The sky was so blue it might have been painted overhead with a brush. Clouds were decorative puffs. And the breeze that sent whorls of dust up and down the street was already warm.

Rose walked toward town. She walked toward the hardware store, to be more precise. The tiny doll dangled around her neck from a harness Sam had made out of one of his leather shoestrings.

Regina had been talking about going to see "her" house since Rose had opened her eyes that morning. Once the princess got an idea into her head, there was no ignoring her.

Not that Rose wasn't glad to see the dollhouse, too. She was, though a dollhouse wasn't the kind of thing she had ever cared about before Regina. (That was the way she thought about her life these days—before and after Regina.)

As she walked along, Rose thought about letting Regina explore the dollhouse this time. After all, Mr. Hines, the owner, rarely came to the back of the store.

Maybe she could explore just the bedroom. That was Regina's favorite. It was frilly and pretty, very much like Rose's room. The bed even had a ruffled pink canopy and spread like the ones on Rose's bed. The walls were scattered with pink rosebuds, too. If the furniture had been white and gold instead of brown, it would have been Rose's room exactly.

The frills suited the princess. Sometimes Rose wished they suited her half as well. As she walked, she tried to imagine turning into the kind of girl who would fit such a room. The kind of girl her mother wanted.

You never know, she told herself. *I might be different someday.*

She was even feeling a little bit different now. Leaving Mr. Simmons's classroom had been like climbing out of her own stuffy trunk. She could breathe. Why, she hadn't mislaid Regina for more than a week. Maybe she would never lose her again. Maybe nothing bad would ever happen again!

And that was what Rose was thinking that fine summer day as she skipped to the back of the store. How beautiful the day was. How nice the world was. How happy she was to be alive on this beautiful day, in this nice world.

Even how glad she was to be the servant of a tiny china princess.

But that was before she came to the shelf where the dollhouse had always stood. The empty shelf where the dollhouse had always stood.

Rose stopped. Her heart plummeted.

What was going on?

Her hand flew to gather in the princess hanging around her neck to protect her from the sight.

But Regina had already seen the empty shelf. "Where is it?" she cried in an accusing voice, as if Rose were the one who had spirited the house away. "What's happened to my house?"

"I—I don't know," Rose stammered. "It was

right here yesterday. Wasn't it yesterday we were here? Anyway, I know it was right here the last time we came."

"We didn't come yesterday," Regina informed her. "Don't you remember? Yesterday you made dandelion soup. And then you wanted to wade in the creek and climb the oak tree. We didn't come to the store at all!"

She said all this in the same accusing tone, as though Rose had insisted on doing things that she, Regina, hadn't wanted to do, which wasn't the case at all. She even rolled her eyes as she spoke, the way some other girls Rose knew liked to do. Her sapphire blue eyes rolled up and away as if to share something bad about Rose with the ceiling. Her rolling eyes said very clearly that Rose was strange, that she was dumb, that she was wrong in every way.

And faster than it takes to tell you, all the

good feeling that had been singing through Rose's veins vanished. It disappeared as completely as the dollhouse had.

"Where is it?" Princess Regina said again in a very loud voice.

Rose tightened her hand around the doll. Not to protect her this time, but to keep her quiet. Why was she taking this silly thing with her everyplace she went, anyway? She was no princess! She was nothing more than another eye-rolling girl.

Rose pulled the leather shoestring from around her neck. Letting Princess Regina dangle from her hand in a most undignified manner, she stomped toward the front of the store. She pushed through the door and onto the summer sidewalk.

And that was when she came face to face with Dumb and Meanie.

"It's Rosie!" Dumb exclaimed. "What a surprise!"

(No one *ever* called her Rosie except Sam, and big brothers have special permission when it comes to pet names. Girls who sit in front of you in class but don't know a single true thing about you do *not* have that same permission.)

Rose started to turn away. She wasn't stuck in a seat in school. She didn't have to pay the slightest attention to this pair! But before she could take two steps, Meanie blocked her. Her eyes were hard on the tiny doll at the end of the leather shoestring.

"Look, Dawn!" Meanie said. "Do you see what Rosie has? A dolly!"

Now, Rose wasn't embarrassed to be found with a "dolly." She didn't care about that at all. But in the few moments it had taken to see that the dollhouse was gone and the few more to walk back out into the June sun, a firestorm had built up in her belly.

She didn't want to be responsible for a tiny china doll who walked and talked . . . and rolled her eyes. She didn't want to watch over her day and night. She didn't want to listen to her or try to please her.

It was hard enough just being herself without having somebody else to worry about.

Rose leaned into the girls. "But she's not just a *dolly*," she said. "Don't you know?" She dangled Regina up in front of their faces. "She's a real princess. So unless you want to be good and sorry, you'd better start bowing."

Then she gave the tiny doll a shake at the end of her leather shoestring and commanded, "Talk for them, Regina. Show them the kind of princess you are!"

Rose knew better, of course. She understood

that the only protection Regina could have in this too-curious world was for as few people as possible to know that she was awake. She understood especially that Regina needed to stay hidden from girls like these. Even so, the moment might have ended there, with Dawn and Melanie laughing—which is what they were doing—if Rose had walked away. It would have been a humiliating walk, but humiliation can be survived.

However, Rose's brain was buzzing, and her skin was popping. And at that moment, she no longer cared what happened to Regina.

She shook the shoestring again. She shook it hard so Regina danced up and down in the air. And she ordered, "Say something, princess. Give us one of your famous commands!"

You might think, as good as she was at ignoring orders, that Regina would have ignored this one, but she didn't. As Melanie reached for her, Regina kicked her pink-clad feet and cried in her shrill voice, "Ding-dong drat it! Don't you dare touch me! I'm a princess, don't you know?"

Everything stopped.

When a storyteller says "everything stopped," we usually mean that every character in the scene went silent. And they did do that, Rose, Dawn, Melanie . . . even Regina after her outburst. But this stopping was so deep, so complete, that for several long seconds the air itself seemed to hold its breath.

And then . . . pandemonium broke loose. (Do you know what *pandemonium* is? If not, perhaps you should look it up. You might learn not just what the word means, but where it comes from.)

Once more Melanie grabbed for the doll. This time she got hold of her and jerked the leather shoestring out of Rose's hand.

Princess Regina let out a muffled screech.

Dawn reached for her, too. "Let me have her! I want her!"

Rose realized all too late what she had done. "Stop!" she yelled.

No one did.

"You've got to stop!" Rose yelled again.

The girls paid no attention. They were playing tug-of-war with the leather shoestring.

"Please!" Rose cried. "Stop!"

"STOP!" came another voice entirely. That last *STOP!* was bellowed so loudly that a bank robber running off with his loot probably would have obeyed.

In any case, everyone stopped and turned to the new voice.

Sam moved toward them with long, loose strides.

Melanie's hand, grasping the tiny china doll,

drifted to her side as though she were holding nothing, as though she had meant nothing.

Sam stepped between Rose and the other girls. "What are you doing?" he asked. The question sifted down quietly from his great height.

"Nothing," Melanie squeaked.

"It didn't look like nothing to me," Sam said. He held out his hand. Without a word, Melanie handed Regina over.

"It's about time," the princess said when she was safe in Sam's hand. But he gave her a look that said, as clearly as any words, *Not now!*

She went silent again.

Rose threw her arms around her brother's waist.

"Have you been playing tricks again, Rosie?" he asked. He pried her arms loose and tucked Regina into her hand. "Did you convince these girls that this little doll can talk?"

Rose caught on instantly. That was the way things were between Rose and Sam. They understood one another.

"It was just a game," she said, ducking her head as if she was ashamed. And the truth is she was. She knew how close she'd come to disaster. "I was teasing them a bit . . . that's all."

"A bit?" Sam chuckled. "That will be the day." He winked at Melanie and Dawn as though including them in a good joke. "My little sister never does things by bits. Now, Rose," he went on. He cupped a hand over her shoulder and turned her to face the girls. "I want you to show your friends how you do it. Talk for the dolly and make us think she's real."

For the briefest of seconds Rose hesitated. Would Melanie and Dawn really believe her if she pretended to talk for the doll the way she had done once with Sam?

Still, she sat Regina on her palm, held her up in front of her face, and said in her best little mouse voice, "Ding-dong drat it! Don't you dare touch me! I'm a princess, don't you know?"

The look on the girls' faces kept shifting. First they looked confused. Then angry. Then admiring. To Rose's surprise, they seemed to buy her little puppet show. Mostly now, they

were embarrassed over having been tricked. But she could tell that they were impressed, too.

"Come on, Rosie," Sam said. He didn't wait for Dawn and Melanie—Dumb and Meanie—to gather themselves enough to start asking questions. "Let's go home."

Like any good storyteller, however, Rose didn't want to leave without finishing her story. She rolled her eyes to the June sky as though Sam were some kind of a nuisance who had interrupted her fun. Only then did she fall into step beside her big brother.

Half a block away, she paused once to wave good-bye. She used the doll to wave with, holding her high so her golden hair and pink gown flashed in the summer sun.

The touch of admiration held long enough for Melanie and Dawn to wave back.

Chapter 9

Zoey

Neither Sam nor Rose spoke as they walked toward home. Even Regina was silent, dangling from the loop of leather shoestring safely in place once more around Rose's neck.

"That was a close call," Sam said finally.

"I know," Rose said. And then she added, "I'm sorry."

It was Sam's turn to say "I know." He might have added, "You're always sorry," but he didn't. That was the kind of big brother Sam was.

He did add something else, though. "You've got to keep Regina safe," he reminded her. "She's got no one except you."

"Yeah!" Regina chimed in. "That's your job . . . keeping me safe."

Sam went on, ignoring the bossy doll. "She's not like us," he said. "If she gets hurt, she can't heal like we can. She can't even grow."

Rose stopped walking for an instant, startled by the idea. The princess couldn't grow. She would always be three and one-quarter inches tall. She couldn't heal, either. If she got chipped or broken, she would be chipped or broken forever.

And she didn't seem to learn the way growing people did. She would never be any different than she was at this moment, bossy and self-centered and . . . was she scared? Was it possible the tiny princess was scared? Rose knew that she would be scared if she were so tiny in such an enormous world.

The doll suddenly felt heavy at the end of her leather harness. Rose lifted the shoestring away from her neck, but then she let Regina fall back into place over her heart again.

Forever. It was a big word. She would be taking care of Princess Regina forever.

They had walked another block before Sam said, "I had a reason for coming for you. I've got something for you."

"Something for me?" Princess Regina cried.

Rose was still too caught in *forever* to respond, but she came alert when Sam said, "Something for both of you."

Regina danced at the end of her leather harness, and even Rose's steps lightened a bit.

Sam would help her with forever. And his surprises were always good!

Rose cupped her palm beneath Regina to give her a softer ride.

"Hey," the princess said. "Get your hand away. I can't see!"

Rose let her hand fall away. Regina truly was a prickly little thing. But it was okay. Rose understood prickly.

Sam led the way up the walk to their yellow house. He led the way through the front door and up the stairs to Rose's room. He pushed the door open and stepped back, bowing.

"Your High Royalnesses," he said, "enter your kingdom."

Rose entered. At first she saw nothing, only what she had left behind when she'd gone downstairs for breakfast that morning. An unmade bed. A tumble of clothes on the floor. (Her mother always told her to put her dirty clothes in the hamper in the bathroom, but somehow they never got there.) Some books and toys scattered here and there.

But then . . . there it was. Rose didn't know how she had missed seeing it when she stepped into the room. She gasped and Regina squealed.

"My house!" Regina cried.

And Rose said, "It's here!"

Here, indeed, it was. The dollhouse that had once been on the shelf in the back of the hardware store now sat on the window seat in Rose's room. Sometimes when you bring something home from the store, it seems to get smaller on the trip home. In Rose's room, the dollhouse had grown more grand.

"Take me to it!" Regina ordered. "This instant!"

So Rose did. She tiptoed across the room, removed Princess Regina from her harness, and set her down very gently in the dollhouse bedroom.

And oh . . . the bedroom!

Not only did the dollhouse look fine there in Rose's room, but the little bedroom had been transformed. It had always been remarkably like Rose's own, with the ruffled pink canopy and pink bedspread on the bed and its scattering of rosebuds on the walls. Now it was *exactly* like hers.

The brown furniture had been painted white with delicate gold trim!

"You?" Rose asked, turning to her brother. "You did this for Regina . . . for me?"

"For both of you," Sam said. "I thought she'd be safe here. And I figured she wouldn't need you so much if she had her own house."

"Need her?" Regina bounced on the bed. She bounced so high her head nearly bumped the pink canopy. "Why would I need her? I have everything I could possibly want right here!"

Rose stepped back, away from the doll-house. "You mean," she said to Regina, "you want to stay here?"

"Of course!" Princess Regina said. She skipped over to the tiny dressing table and sat in front of the oval mirror. "Now and then, perhaps," she said, "you can take me out to my throne room . . . or for a walk in the woods. As for going into town and meeting those nasty girls"—her tiny shoulders shuddered—"who needs it? I'll stay right here, thank you very much."

"If you're sure," Rose said, though she wasn't at all sure herself. Was this what *she* wanted?

Sam, however, seemed pleased. "Sounds good to me," he said. "Let's get some lunch." And he headed for the stairs.

Rose followed, but slowly.

She stopped in the doorway, looking back. Princess Regina still sat in front of the mirror, arranging her hair, smoothing a wrinkle from her pretty pink gown, examining her flawless china skin.

"Bye," Rose said.

When Regina didn't reply, she said more loudly, "Good-bye, Your Royal Highness!"

Then, without waiting for an answer, she followed Sam downstairs.

It was just as well Rose didn't wait, because the princess didn't bother to answer. After all, a princess isn't obligated to speak every time she is spoken to.

She gathered her golden hair in both hands and held it up. Should she wear it this way? She let it fall. Or that?

After a few minutes and a few different hairstyles, she got up and crossed the room to look through the dollhouse window. From there she could see out the larger window in Rose's room into the yard. That was good. If she got bored, she could always look out the window.

Not that she expected to get bored.

She did wish she could go into the other rooms, though. Unfortunately, the dollhouse wasn't designed that way. There was no stairway, not even doors between the rooms. She needed a human hand to move her from room to room through the open front.

And that was a problem, too. Why was the front of the house open? She would never have any privacy. What if she didn't always want her servant watching?

Regina lay down on the bed. She got up. She sat in the graceful velvet chair, then got up from there, too.

She walked to one wall and then to the other. She walked to the window and to the gaping front of the house.

"Maybe," she said to herself and to the empty room beyond her cozy dollhouse, "it would be all right if Rose came back . . . just for a little while."

She sat on the window seat, smoothed her satin skirt, crossed her ankles prettily, and waited.

The girl, the big, clumsy girl, would return. Whatever mistakes Rose made along the way, she always came back.

Rose did come back, of course. It was, after all, her room, her dollhouse, her doll. Not to mention her responsibility. But not for several hours.

Sam kept her busy all afternoon.

After lunch he suggested a bicycle ride. Sam was the one who had taught Rose to ride her bike, but he'd never before asked her to ride with him. "Your legs are too short, pip-squeak," he'd say. "You can't keep up."

This day, though, he said, "How about we get our bikes out and go for a ride."

And they did.

He kept pace alongside her, too, never riding out ahead. He didn't call her pip-squeak, either . . . except once when she had to stop for the third time on their way up the big hill behind the Methodist church.

After their bike ride, they got ice cream sandwiches from the freezer in the back of the grocery store. And then, to Rose's delight, Sam suggested that they go swimming at the quarry. The quarry was where all the big kids went. Sam had never taken Rose there before.

At the quarry, he held her up when the water was too deep and never called her pip-squeak even once.

It was nice, Rose had to admit to herself, not to have to worry about Regina for a while.

Rose was tired when they got home for supper, but still, she hurried upstairs to see her doll.

She let out a sigh of relief when she stepped into the room. There the princess sat on the window seat inside the dollhouse, looking right at her. Her ankles were crossed neatly, and her tiny hands were folded in her lap.

Everything was fine. Regina even looked happy, sitting there in her own little bedroom.

"Have you been having fun?" Rose asked, crossing to the dollhouse. "I've had the best time. First, Sam and I went biking. We even went up the hill behind . . ."

But her voice trailed off. Princess Regina didn't seem to be listening. In fact, she didn't seem to be doing anything, not even moving.

She was just sitting . . . staring . . . as deaf and dumb as any other china doll.

"Oh!" Rose cried, and she scooped the tiny doll into her hand. "Oh . . . don't! You can't go off to sleep." She shook Regina gently. No response.

This was so unfair. *She* hadn't forgotten this time. Regina had told her to go. The princess had practically dismissed her!

After a moment, Rose laid the doll down very gently on the dollhouse bed and backed away until she bumped into her own bed. She sat down abruptly.

She would not cry! She would *not*!

Rose sat for a long time watching Regina, but she didn't pick her up again. After a while, she wiped away a tear. Only one. There would be no more.

Princess Regina was safe now. The princess

had her own little house, and she was perfectly safe.

To tell the truth, Rose didn't know how to
feel. She was almost as glad as she was sad not
to take care of the princess any longer. She
didn't have to take constant orders. She didn't
have to protect the doll from every kind of

accident. She didn't have to keep her hidden from grabby hands.

But still . . .

Rose cocked her head and studied Regina. The tiny doll's expression had changed since Rose had discovered her. She no longer looked down and away as though avoiding too-friendly hands. She looked directly out into the world like someone who was waiting for something . . . for someone.

And so this story ends. Princess Regina is tucked away in her own house. Rose is free to be Rose, a challenge enough all by itself.

Will Rose ever learn the secret of waking the doll? Or will she wake her accidentally without knowing how it happens?

Either way, if Regina does wake, the two of them are sure to have more adventures, more disagreements. And eventually, because Rose is Rose and because caring for another waking creature is very hard, Regina will be left to sleep again.

Perhaps when Rose grows up, she will even forget about Regina's power to wake. The truth is grown-ups do forget a lot.

But all this lies outside the story I'm telling. A story, any story, contains only the smallest part of a life.

There is one thing that I can tell you for certain will happen, though.

Rose will have a daughter one day, not a china doll but a real baby who breathes and eats and, yes, poops. And Rose's ideas won't be so grand when it comes to naming her. She'll not call her Regina. Queen. She'll go for something shorter, more ordinary.

Like Zoey. Not Princess Zoey. Just Zoey.

It's a good name. *Zoey* means *life*, in case you didn't know. And what is more sweet, more painful, more miraculous than life?

Rose will try hard, very, very hard—though it's an enormously difficult thing to do—to take care of Zoey every minute.

And if Rose is still Rose and can't always manage? Well, her mother, the good Hazel, will be there.

And at Hazel's house a tiny doll will be waiting to waken.